Walt Disney's

Lady

AND THE

TRAMP

WALT DISNEY'S

Lady

AND THE

TRAMP

WALT DISNEY'S
Lady
AND THE
TRAMP

ADAPTED FROM THE FILM BY
TODD STRASSER

DISNEY PRESS

NEW YORK

Library of Congress Catalog Card Number: 93-71379
ISBN: 1-56282-614-X

Walt Disney's

Lady

AND THE

TRAMP

CHAPTER ONE

IT WAS A CHRISTMAS EVE many years ago, and a gentle snow was falling on the town, covering the trees and the rooftops with a smooth white fleece. Groups of carolers sang of good cheer and peace for all, and if you listened carefully you could hear the jingling bells of a horse-drawn sleigh in the distance.

At the end of a lane in a comfortable neighborhood, past a tall iron fence and down a snow-covered path, stood a large wooden house. An evergreen wreath hung from the front door, and through the window could be seen a brightly lit Christmas tree in the living room. Many colorfully wrapped boxes lay in a tumble on the floor beneath it.

A newlywed couple was celebrating their first Christmas together. The husband, a tall, handsome man with a brown mustache, presented his wife with a striped hatbox tied with a ribbon.

"For you, Darling," he said. "Merry Christmas."

His wife was thrilled. For weeks she had been admiring a certain hat in the window of the local hat shop.

"Oh, Jim Dear," she said, "it's the one I liked so much, isn't it? The one that's trimmed with ribbons?"

She opened the box and gasped. Out popped the most adorable cocker spaniel puppy the woman had ever seen. A red bow was tied around the puppy's neck.

"Well, she *does* have a ribbon," Jim Dear said with a chuckle.

"Oh, what a sweet surprise!" his wife cried happily as she picked up the puppy.

"Do you like her, Darling?" Jim asked. Perhaps, he worried to himself, she might have wanted the hat more, after all?

"Oh, Jim Dear, I love her," Darling said. She hugged the puppy, who licked her face. "What a perfectly beautiful little lady."

The evening passed, and Darling and Jim Dear opened the rest of their presents. But it was clear that Lady was their favorite. They played with her until it was time to go to bed.

"Where will she sleep?" Darling asked with a yawn.

"I'll show you." Jim Dear led her into the kitchen, where a brand-new basket with a soft white cushion lay on the floor. "Come on, Lady. Over here."

Lady eagerly followed her new owners through the door and slid to a stop on the polished kitchen floor.

"That's a girl," Jim Dear said as he picked her up and placed her in the basket. "There now, a nice little bed for you."

"But Jim Dear, are you sure she'll be warm enough?" Darling asked as she spread a little blanket over the puppy.

"Why, of course, Darling. She'll be snug as a bug in a rug." Jim Dear turned down the gaslight and was about to say "Good night, Lady" when he stopped. "Oh, oh. Almost forgot." He spread out some news-paper on the floor next to Lady's basket.

He patted Lady gently on the head. "Now, good night, Lady."

Jim Dear noticed at once the worried expression on his wife's face. "Don't worry, Darling," he assured her. "She'll go right to sleep."

But Lady didn't want to sleep. No sooner had the kitchen door swung shut than Lady hopped out of the basket and pushed open the kitchen door with her paw. She scampered into the hallway. Jim Dear and Darling were nearly at the top of the stairs. Lady yelped.

"Oh, look," Darling said. "She's lonesome. Don't you think," she asked, "that maybe, just for tonight, she could stay with us?"

Jim Dear frowned and clumped down the stairs. Lady wagged her tail happily.

"Now, Darling," he explained as he picked Lady up. "If we're going to show Lady who's master, we must be firm from the very beginning." He took Lady back to the kitchen and again put her in the basket. "This is where you belong, Lady," he said sternly. "Right here."

Lady let him tuck her in. But as soon as Jim Dear was gone, she jumped out of the basket again. She pushed at the kitchen door with her paw, but this time the door would not open. She pushed again. How strange, Lady thought. She peered under the door. A chair had been set against it. Lady was confused. They didn't really expect her to *sleep* in this cold, dark kitchen all night, did they?

Lady started to yip and cry. A moment later she was startled by a banging sound coming from upstairs. "Lady!" Jim Dear shouted, "Stop that. *Now!*"

Lady stood at the kitchen door and cried some more. Finally, she heard the clomping of footsteps coming down the stairs. A light went on, and Lady saw a shadow appear under the doorway.

"Quiet now!" Jim Dear shouted to Lady from the other side of the door. "You hear me? Back to bed. Quick now. Not one more sound."

Lady sadly went back to her basket.

She tried to sleep, but the loud ticks and chimes of the clock made it impossible. An hour dragged by. Finally, Lady crawled out of her basket and trotted back to the kitchen door. She pushed and pushed until finally it opened. She ran down the hall. The stairs loomed before her like a steep mountain. Lady had never climbed stairs before.

Lady stumbled up the stairs as best she could. She paused for a moment on the landing to catch her breath, then bounded into a room where she thought she might find Jim Dear and Darling. A loud snorting sound frightened her, but it was only Jim Dear snoring. Lady pawed at the covers and howled.

"Jim Dear . . . ," she heard Darling whisper.

"Hmmm . . ." Jim Dear rolled over and pulled a pillow over his head. Lady howled again.

"Aw, Jim," Darling said plaintively.

"Uh, what, what?" Jim Dear mumbled sleepily.

"Look," Darling said.

Jim Dear leaned over the edge of the bed and let out a big sigh. "Oh, all right," he said, reaching down for Lady. He set her down at the foot of the bed. Darling covered her with a soft blanket, and Lady settled snugly into her new, warm bed.

"But remember," Jim Dear warned, "it's just for tonight!"

CHAPTER TWO

HALF A YEAR'S WORTH of "just for tonights" later, Lady was still sleeping snugly at the foot of the bed. It was summer now, and Lady was nearly full grown. She loved taking early morning strolls with Jim Dear before he went to work, then playing outside all day while Darling did her chores.

One morning the clock's chime woke Lady as usual. She stretched and felt hungry. It was time to tug at Jim Dear's pajamas until he got up and fed her.

"All right, Lady, all right," Jim Dear muttered with a yawn. "I'm up, Lady." He groaned. "Oh no!"

"What is it, Jim?" Darling asked. "What's wrong?"

Jim Dear flopped back down on the bed. "Can't you explain to Lady about Sundays?"

Lady watched Jim Dear crawl back under the covers. Oh well, Lady thought. If he was too tired to give her breakfast now, she could wait. It was a beautiful day, and there was so much to see and do outside. She raced down the stairs, ran into the kitchen, and climbed through the small door Jim Dear had built so she could come and go as she pleased.

Outside, the air was fresh and sweet. Lady saw a small flock of blackbirds on the lawn and chased them into the air. She ran into the backyard and found an old bone in the grass. She knew the perfect place to bury it, too. In the garden near the woodpile she dug a small hole, dropped in the bone, and neatly patted down the dirt. She also dug up a pink tulip and replanted it upside down.

"There," she said, and smiled.

Just then Lady heard a faint scratching sound. Curious, Lady went to investigate. Suddenly, from inside the woodpile, a rat poked out its head. It had sharp pointed teeth and mean, tiny red eyes. Lady barked, but the rat grinned smugly as if to say, "You don't frighten me." Lady sprang at the rat, and it turned and ran. Lady chased it across the yard, but the rat slipped through a hole in the fence. Lady tried to squeeze under the fence, but the hole was too small for her. She clawed frantically at the dirt.

Just then a bicycle bell rang out in the street. The newspaper boy! Lady quickly forgot about the rat and raced to the front of the house just as the Sunday paper landed with a THWACK on the walk. The Sunday paper was always much heavier than the daily, and as Lady lugged it through the doggy door it ripped.

Jim Dear and Darling were having breakfast in the kitchen. Jim Dear took the paper from Lady. "Thank you, Lady," he said. As a reward Darling gave her a doughnut. Lady sat down happily and watched Jim Dear spread out the paper.

"Have you noticed, Darling," he said with a chuckle, peering at his wife through a large hole in the paper, "that ever since we got Lady we've seen less and less of those disturbing headlines?"

"Yes," Darling said, patting Lady affectionately on the head. "I don't know how we ever got along without her."

"It's been only six months," Jim Dear said. He put the paper down for a moment. "That reminds me. Isn't it time to get Lady a license?"

Lady perked up her ears.

"You're right," said Darling. "I'll get it tomorrow."

The next day Darling showed Lady a white box tied with a pink ribbon.

"Here's a present for you," she said, taking out a beautiful blue collar with a shiny diamond-shaped tag. "I hope it fits."

Lady wagged her tail excitedly as Darling slipped the collar around her neck. She held a mirror in front of Lady so that she could admire her reflection.

"My, but it does look nice," Darling said. "And so grown up! Won't Jock and Trusty be surprised."

Lady was thrilled. *Her own license!* She dashed out the front door and ran to the large redbrick house across the street.

She found her friend Jock, a black Scottie, busily engaged in the business of burying a bone.

"Hello, lassie," Jock said when he saw Lady.

Lady pranced proudly around him. "Notice anything different?" she asked.

Jock frowned. "You've had a bath?"

"No, not that," Lady said. "Something else."

"Er, you've had your nails clipped?"

"Guess again," Lady said playfully.

"Well, I, I wouldn't be knowing," Jock said apologetically. Lady shook her head so the license jingled. Jock smiled proudly. "Why, lassie, a bonny new collar."

"Do you like it?" Lady asked.

"Aye." Jock nodded and sniffed. "Hmm, it smells very expensive. Have you shown it to Trusty yet?"

Lady shook her head.

"Then we'd best go at once," Jock said. "You know how sensitive he is about these things."

They strolled through the neighborhood until they came to a large old manor house with tall white columns covered with vines. Trusty lay sleeping on the front porch. As Lady and Jock came up the walk, the old brown bloodhound twitched and snorted in his sleep.

"He's dreaming," Lady whispered.

"Aye," Jock whispered back. "Dreaming of those bonny bygone days when he and his grandfather tracked criminals through the swamps."

Lady looked at Jock with wide eyes. "I didn't know he did that."

"Aye," Jock nodded solemnly. "But that was . . . before."

"Before what?" Lady asked.

" 'Tis time you knew the truth," Jock said with a tragic sigh. "It shouldn't have happened to a dog, but Trusty has lost his sense of smell."

"Oh, how sad!" Lady said.

"Aye," Jock agreed. "But we must never let on that we know, lassie. It would break his poor heart."

Just then Trusty woke from his nap and saw his friends. "Why, hello, Miss Lady," Trusty said with a yawn. "Hello, Jock."

"Notice something new?" Lady asked, shaking the collar.

"Why, Miss Lady, you have a collar!" said Trusty admiringly.

"And a license," Lady added proudly.

10

"My my, how time does fly," Trusty said wistfully.

"Aye," Jock said. "It seems like only yesterday she was cuttin' her teeth on Jim Dear's slippers. And now, here she is, a full-grown Lady."

"Wearin' the greatest honor humans can bestow," Trusty intoned gravely.

"The badge of faith and respectability," said Jock solemnly.

"He's right, Miss Lady," Trusty said. "As my grand-pappy, Old Reliable, used to say . . ." He paused. "Don't recollect if I've ever mentioned Old Reliable before."

Jock nodded wearily. "Aye, you have, laddie."

Trusty frowned. "I have? Hmmm." He seemed a bit puzzled. Then, in the distance, Lady heard a whistle.

"It's Jim Dear," she said quickly, turning to go. "Home from work. Please excuse me." Lady raced down the block. Jim Dear was just turning the corner on his way home.

"Well, what have we here?" Jim Dear said as Lady came running up the walk. He reached down to touch the small diamond-shaped license. "So, you're a big girl now, huh? All right, Lady, how about some dinner?" He held open the door for her. "Ladies first," he said.

Later that evening Darling and Jim Dear sat by the fire. Lady lay on the floor, admiring her license as it twinkled in the firelight.

11

"You know, Darling," Jim Dear said, puffing contentedly on his pipe and patting Lady lightly on the head. "With Lady here, I'd say life is quite complete."

Darling looked up from her knitting and smiled. "Yes, dear. I don't imagine anything could ever take her place."

CHAPTER THREE

NOT FAR AWAY in a neighborhood of dirt alleys and smoky factories, a happy-go-lucky mutt named Tramp woke up in a barrel beside the train yards.

Ah, what a beautiful morning, he thought as he stretched and yawned. He took a leisurely sip of water from a puddle on the ground and washed his grayish brown fur under a leaking water tower. His stomach rumbled. Time to find breakfast, Tramp decided.

To Tramp, having no home and no owner was the only way to live. How else could a dog get to sample all the fabulous cuisines the world had to offer? As he strolled down the cobblestoned street, he considered the breakfast possibilities. Bernie's Grill? No, he had eaten there last night. What about those delicious cakes and petits fours in the window of François Pastries? Better not—a dog who lived by his wits had to watch his weight.

Then Tramp spotted Tony's Restaurant. Perfect! He hadn't been there in a week. He turned down the alley and scratched on the back door. Joe, the chef, opened it.

"*Buon giorno, Butch!*" he said with a big smile. "You want some breakfast, huh?"

Tramp jumped up and down and barked eagerly.

"Okay," Joe said. "The boss, he saved some nice bones for you. Breakfast coming up from left field!" He tossed a bone out the door. Tramp leapt in the air and caught it. "Good catch!"

Tramp found a cozy spot behind a nearby fence and sat down contentedly to enjoy his breakfast. But he wasn't even halfway through the delicious meal when he was distracted by the disturbing but familiar clumping of a horse-drawn wagon. Tramp peeked through a hole in the fence and immediately recognized the dark green wagon. Even worse, caged in the back of the wagon were his two good friends Bull, an English bulldog, and Peg, a blue-eyed Pekingese.

The dogcatcher had stopped his wagon and was hammering a sign onto the fence. As soon as the man turned away, Tramp slipped around and took a look.

WARNING:
NOTICE IS HEREBY GIVEN
THAT ANY UNLICENSED DOG
WILL BE IMMEDIATELY IMPOUNDED.
—BY ORDER OF THE CITY COUNCIL

Wow, Tramp thought, the city's really cracking down. The dogcatcher had gone down the block to post another sign, and Tramp tiptoed over to the wagon.

"Hey," he whispered.

From inside the cage, Bull turned and looked surprised. "Blimey! Look, Peg, it's Tramp!"

Peg strolled over to the latched wire door and winked. "Hi, handsome. Come to join the party?"

"No time for wisecracks," Tramp said, reaching toward the latch. "Looks like the pressure's really on. There are signs all over town."

Tramp nudged the latch, and the door swung open.

"Gee, thanks," Peg said.

"You're a bit of all right," said Bull appreciatively. Tramp would have liked to stay and chat, but just then the dogcatcher came bundling up the street.

"Get going, you two," Tramp said quickly as he ducked under the wagon. "Scram! And be careful!"

His two friends jumped from the wagon and ran. "Hey!" shouted the dogcatcher as he caught sight of them. "What's going on over there?" The dogcatcher grabbed his net. But just as he swung out at Peg and Bull with it, Tramp jumped out from under the wagon and bit into the cuff of his pants.

"Hey!" Startled, the dogcatcher spun around. "Why, you mangy mutt," he said, recognizing Tramp. "Let go of me!"

Tramp let go and ran.

"I'll get you for this!" the dogcatcher shouted.

Tramp ran as fast as he could, but the dogcatcher was gaining on him. He'd saved his friends. Now he had to save himself.

CHAPTER FOUR

JOCK AND TRUSTY decided it was the perfect day to call on Lady.

"Lassie! Lassie!" Jock called out as they strolled across Lady's front lawn.

"Oh, Miss Lady, ma'am," Trusty bellowed. "Miss Lady!"

It was odd that Lady didn't answer, Jock thought. He and Trusty went around to the back. There they found her, lying in the shade by her food dish.

"Ah, good morning, lassie," Jock said with an enthusiastic wag of his tail. " 'Tis a bonny bright day."

Lady sighed and gave Jock a sorrowful look.

17

"Why, Miss Lady," Trusty said, furrowing his brow. "Is something wrong?"

"Aye," said Jock. "Tell us, lassie. If someone's been mistreating you—"

Lady quickly looked up. "Oh, it's nothing like that. It's something I've done . . . I guess."

"*You,* Miss Lady?" said Trusty with an astonished look.

"It must be," Lady said. "Jim Dear and Darling are acting so strange."

They were too close to the house to talk privately, so Jock suggested they join him behind the greenhouse, where they wouldn't be disturbed.

"Now, lassie," Jock said finally. "Get on with the details."

Lady told them her story. She'd first noticed that something was different a few days before when she went to greet Jim Dear as he came home from work. As soon as she had seen him walking down the sidewalk, she burst out of the house and ran down the steps to give him a big hello.

"Usually he's so happy to see me," Lady said in an injured tone. "But instead he walked right past and said, 'Down, Lady, down!' " Jock shook his head. "He's never done that before," she added.

Jock gave Trusty a worried look. "All right, lassie, continue," Jock said.

Lady told them how Jim Dear had rushed into the

house calling for Darling and asking if she was all right. He'd said something about Darling's condition—alone in the house all day and having to walk *that dog.*

Jock was shocked. *"That dog?"* he repeated.

Lady sniffed. "He's never called me that before."

"Now, now, lassie," Jock said gently. "I wouldn't worry about that. Remember, they're only humans, after all."

Trusty nodded. "As my grandpappy, Old Reliable, used to say . . ." He paused. "Don't recollect if I've ever mentioned Old Reliable before."

"Aye, ya have, laddy," Jock said a bit irritably. "Frequently."

"But there's more," Lady said. She told them how, the day before, she'd carried her leash to Darling for her regular afternoon walk, but Darling refused to go out.

"Why?" Jock asked.

"I don't know," Lady said. "She just sat there, knitting tiny pink socks."

Jock and Trusty looked at each other.

"Tiny pink socks?" Jock asked.

"Uh-huh," Lady said.

"Go on, lassie," Jock said.

Lady explained how she had tried to interest Darling in a game, but Darling didn't want to play. When the ball of pink yarn rolled off Darling's lap, Lady thought it would be fun to play with it, so she picked it up in her mouth and ran. But Darling chased after her and spanked her on the bottom.

Jock gasped. "Spanked you?"

"It didn't hurt, really," Lady admitted. "But Darling never struck me before."

"Now, lassie," Jock said in a gently soothing tone. "Don't take it too seriously. After all, at a time like this . . ."

"A time like what?" she asked, puzzled.

Trusty tried to explain. "There comes a time in the life of most humans when, uh, er, as they put it, the birds and the bees."

Lady was more confused than ever.

"What Trusty's trying to say," Jock blurted, "is that Darling is expecting a baby."

"Oh." Lady frowned. She blinked once or twice, then asked, "What's a baby?"

"Babies resemble humans," Jock explained.

"But they're a mite bit smaller," Trusty added. "And if I remember correctly, they cry a lot."

"They walk on all fours," said Jock. "And they're *very* expensive. You'll not be permitted to play with it."

"But they're mighty sweet," Trusty countered.

"And very, very soft," agreed Jock.

It was just then that Tramp strolled by. The dogcatcher had chased him all the way from one side of town to the other. But he'd finally gotten away.

Tramp couldn't help but notice that the cocker spaniel was a real knockout. And he could see that these two old fogies didn't have a clue as to what babies were really about.

"Babies are a regular bundle of . . . trouble," he said, trotting up to them and boldly interrupting.

Jock and Trusty looked startled as Tramp squeezed his way in next to Lady.

"Babies may be sweet," he explained to Lady, "but they also scratch, pinch, and pull ears. And that's not the worst of it. It's what they do to your happy home." He paused significantly, then continued. "Home wreckers, that's what they are."

"Look here, laddie," Jock barked angrily. "Who are you to barge in?"

"The voice of experience," Tramp replied confidently. "Just wait until Junior gets here," he told Lady. "You get the urge for a nice comfortable scratch, and suddenly everyone's shouting that you'll get fleas on the baby. You feel like barking at some strange mutt, and they yell at you for waking up the baby." He gave Lady a disgusted weary-of-the-world look. "And wait until they hit you in the room-and-board department. You know those nice juicy cuts of beef they feed you?"

Lady nodded.

"Forget it," Tramp said with a dismissive wave of his paw. "From now on it's leftover baby food. And you know that nice warm bed by the fire? Once Junior gets here it'll be a cold, damp doghouse for you."

Lady gasped at the thought. A doghouse?

"Don't listen to him, lassie," Jock said. "No human is *that* cruel."

"That's right, Miss Lady," Trusty said. "Everybody knows a dog's best friend is his human."

Tramp couldn't help laughing. "Come on, fellas, you haven't fallen for that old line," he said.

"Aye," Jock snapped, "and we've no need for mongrels and their radical ideas!" He'd had enough of this ill-kept, insolent troublemaker. "Now off with you! Go away!"

Tramp figured that the Scottie meant business. "Okay, Sandy," he said agreeably.

"The name's Jock. Now go!"

"Okay, okay," said Tramp, pulling together his dignity as best he could. "I'm going." He turned to leave. "Just remember," he warned Lady, "a human heart has only so much room for love and affection. When a baby moves in, the dog moves out."

He trotted off the lawn and disappeared. Lady was dumbfounded. Could he be right? she wondered. Could Jim Dear and Darling ever do anything like that to her?

CHAPTER FIVE

WINTER CAME and spring followed, and Jim Dear and Darling continued to behave quite strangely. They had endless discussions about names and spent hours fixing up a room that no one lived in. Odder still was the way Darling's stomach grew and how she would send Jim Dear out in the middle of the night for strange combinations of food, like watermelon and chop suey.

Worst of all, they were so preoccupied that Lady sometimes thought they'd forgotten about her completely.

Then one stormy April night Jim Dear called the doctor in a panic. There was a terrific commotion upstairs, and Lady feared at first that Darling was ill. But then Jim Dear came down babbling about a boy. The *baby* had arrived!

In the days that followed Lady could hear the baby crying upstairs in the nursery. In the kitchen she saw the bottles he drank from, and outside, things called *diapers* hung from the clothesline. Everyone went around smiling and happy.

Everyone, that is, but Lady. She would have been happy, too, if anyone paid attention to her. But nobody did.

One day Lady's curiosity got the better of her. She quietly climbed the stairs and pushed open the door to the nursery. Inside, Darling was singing a lullaby to something cradled in her arms and wrapped snugly in blankets. As Darling placed the bundle in the cradle, Lady cautiously rose on her hind legs and tried to look in.

Suddenly Jim Dear came up behind her. Lady ducked down, frightened that he would be angry with her for coming into the nursery. But Jim Dear gently lifted her up, and Darling turned back the blankets. There was a tiny pink person with hardly any hair on his head.

Lady was surprised. This is a baby? she thought. This is what Jim Dear and Darling spend so much time fussing over?

Still, Jock and Trusty were right. The baby did look soft, and he smelled so sweet. Lady couldn't help liking him. Then she had the nicest surprise. Jim Dear patted her head, and Darling scratched her behind the ear. Lady was happy again. They hadn't forgotten her after all.

Summer came and went, and Lady visited the baby every day. She loved to watch him play and grow. Soon the baby was moved to a crib. Jim Dear and Darling rarely left their son alone, but whenever they did, Lady stood guard outside the nursery to make sure he was safe.

One evening Lady was startled to find Jim Dear packing a suitcase.

"Ready, Darling?" he called into the nursery.

Lady ran into the nursery and found Darling rocking the crib. Jim Dear came in.

"We haven't much time, Darling," he reminded his wife. "We have to leave."

"Oh, Jim," Darling said. "I just can't leave him. He's still so small and helpless."

"Come on," Jim insisted. "If he wakes up, we'll never get away."

Darling rose reluctantly. "I feel so guilty deserting him."

"Nonsense," Jim said, taking her by the arm and guiding her into the hall. Lady was shocked. Deserting the baby! This was no way for them to behave! They must have lost their senses! She stopped them at the top of the stairs.

"What's the matter with Lady?" Jim Dear asked.

"She thinks we're running out on him," Darling said.

Jim Dear bent down to give Lady a reassuring pat, but she pulled away. "Don't worry, Lady," he promised. "We'll be back in a few days."

"Aunt Sarah will be here to watch the baby," Darling said.

"And we know you'll be a big help," Jim Dear said.

That was more like it. Now Lady let him pet her— as long as they were coming back soon and someone was coming to stay with the baby.

The doorbell rang downstairs. Jim Dear straightened up.

"There's the old girl now," he said, starting down the stairs. "Coming, Aunt Sarah," he called out.

Lady followed him. Jim Dear opened the door for a white-haired woman carrying a suitcase and a blue picnic basket.

"Sorry I'm late, dears," she sang out sweetly. "I hope I haven't kept you waiting."

"Not at all." Jim Dear reached for her bags. "Let me help you with your things."

"Now, now, no fussing," Aunt Sarah said. "I know my way around. You better be on your way. Mustn't miss your train. Have a good time, and don't worry about a thing."

She hurried Jim Dear and Darling out the door.

Lady was already feeling a bit lonely. Aunt Sarah hadn't noticed her at all.

"Now," Aunt Sarah said, "I must see that big nephew of mine." Lady followed her upstairs and watched her bend over the crib.

"You adorable little—" Suddenly Aunt Sarah gasped. "Ahh! What are you doing here?" she yelled at Lady. "Go on now!"

Lady blinked in astonishment.

"Get out! Out!" Aunt Sarah shouted. Lady ran from the nursery. The door slammed shut, and inside she could hear the baby starting to cry. "There, there," she heard Aunt Sarah say to the baby. "I won't let that dog frighten you anymore."

Frighten the baby? Lady thought. Why, that was just what Aunt Sarah had done by shouting so loudly! Lady sighed and went back downstairs. When she came into the living room she was surprised to discover two Siamese cats poking up from Aunt Sarah's picnic basket.

The cats, Si and Am, gave Lady a mischievous grin and leapt from the basket.

Curious and a bit suspicious, Lady followed after them and was horrified when they began pulling on the tablecloth with the fishbowl on it. The poor fish was swimming around and around in a panic.

Lady sprang at the cats, but it was too late. The fishbowl teetered on the edge of the table and fell. It hit the floor with a horrifying CRASH. Water splashed everywhere.

The cats grinned slyly from ear to ear. Lady had to

save the poor fish! "What awful beasts!" Lady barked. The cats ran. They leapt onto a table and knocked over a vase. They raked the curtains with their claws. Lady shivered as she heard them rip and tear. *Oh, this is horrible!* Lady barked. *Stop it at once!* Suddenly the baby began to cry. The cats grinned at one another and started up the stairs to the nursery. But Lady jumped ahead and blocked their way, so they shot back down the stairs and into the living room with Lady in mad pursuit. They leapt onto the windowsill and knocked down the drapes. Lady tangled herself up in them and accidentally bumped into a picture stand. There was another loud *CRASH* as a picture frame smashed on the floor.

"What's going on down there?" came the startled voice of Aunt Sarah. Lady was still tangled in the drapes when she heard footsteps on the stairs, then a gasp. "Merciful heavens!"

To Lady's astonishment Aunt Sarah ran to her cats, who were wailing as if Lady had attacked them.

"My darlings!" cooed Aunt Sarah as she scooped the cats up in her arms. "My precious pets!" She paused to survey the damage in the living room. She glared at Lady. "You wicked animal, attacking my poor innocent little angels!"

Lady watched unhappily from under the drapes as Aunt Sarah marched upstairs with a grinning cat under each arm.

CHAPTER SIX

THE NEXT DAY Aunt Sarah called for a taxi and took Lady into town. Lady was excited. She had never been to town before. She carried Lady into a shop filled with all sorts of fish and birds and other creatures. Lady was fascinated.

"How can I help you?" the man behind the counter asked Aunt Sarah.

"I want a muzzle," said Aunt Sarah crisply. "A good strong muzzle."

"Yes, ma'am," the man said. "Here's our latest combination leash and muzzle." He reached toward Lady. "We'll just slip it on like this."

Lady squirmed and jumped back, but the muzzle was

on her face. It was terrible! She had to get it off! She leapt off the counter and started to run.

"Lady, stop now!" Aunt Sarah shouted, reaching for the leash. "Come back!"

But Lady had to get away.

She pulled as hard as she could on the leash. Aunt Sarah stumbled and fell. Free at last, Lady dashed out of the store and into the cobblestoned street.

Beep! Beep! Beep! blared an automobile horn. Confused, Lady jumped as the car roared past. Lady turned to run and just narrowly missed being struck by a bicycle. She dashed this way, and a streetcar rumbled by. She darted that way, and a truck skidded past, leaving her coughing in a cloud of exhaust. Lady had never been more terrified in all her life!

She fled down a side street and tipped over a pile of garbage. There was a terrific commotion as cans and bottles spilled in all directions. Several cans got caught in the leash and rattled behind her like a string of firecrackers. Suddenly Lady heard barking! She turned to look behind her and saw three huge dogs running toward her with bared fangs and wild, savage looks in their eyes. Her heart pounding, Lady turned and ran.

Nearby, Tramp was enjoying a leisurely lunch when he heard barking. It's that gang of dogs, he thought, probably terrorizing some poor cat who's wandered onto their turf. Tramp shook his head and shrugged. Oh well, he thought, it is *just* a cat, after all. Then he

30

saw whom they were chasing. It was *her*—the pretty cocker spaniel from the fancy side of town!

Tramp jumped up and raced after them. The cocker spaniel was headed for a dead-end alley, but Tramp knew a shortcut. He just hoped he could get there in time.

Lady ran for her life. Suddenly she skidded to a stop at the foot of a tall wooden fence. It was far too high to jump over. She looked left and right. The three big dogs were right behind her. Lady sneaked behind a barrel, trembling.

The three dogs leered at Lady with menacing eyes. Slowly they moved toward her.

Suddenly Tramp bounded over the fence and landed between Lady and her attackers. The dogs charged, and there went up a terrible whirlwind of barking and snarling. Lady watched in horror as they bit and snapped, kicking up a cloud of dust and knocking over barrels and garbage cans. Lady had never heard or seen anything as terrifying.

Finally, she heard the three dogs yelping and trotting away in defeat. Lady slowly stuck her head out from behind the barrel. Tramp was strolling back down the alley toward her with a smile on his face.

"Hey," he called as if nothing had happened. "What are you doing on this side of the tracks? I thought you—" He stopped short when he saw the muzzle. "You poor kid! We've got to get that off!"

Lady nodded sadly. "But how can I thank you?" she asked.

"Aw, that was nothing," Tramp said. "The real challenge will be getting that muzzle off you." He thought for a moment. "Hey, I think I know just the place!"

Tramp started to trot out of the alley, and Lady jogged beside him. She wasn't exactly sure if she should trust him. But he *had* saved her life, so it was worth a try.

They walked across town and ducked into the bushes outside the zoo. A large policeman patrolled out front under a sign that read No Dogs Allowed.

Lady peered at the sign, then looked at Tramp. "We can't go in. The sign says—"

Tramp just smiled. "Yeah, well," he said, "that's the angle."

"Angle?" asked Lady.

"Here, you'll see," Tramp said. They waited patiently in the bushes until a man wearing glasses exited the zoo. Much to Lady's surprise, Tramp leapt out from behind the bushes and pretended to be the man's pet. He jumped around and licked the man's hand and wagged his tail. The policeman frowned, pointed to the No Dogs Allowed sign, and began scolding the man. "You can't bring your dog to the zoo," the policeman said. The man replied that he'd done no such thing.

"Are you calling me a liar then?" the policeman demanded of him. They began to argue, and Tramp and Lady slipped past the entrance unnoticed.

"So that's the angle?" Lady asked.

"Yup," Tramp said. "You're catching on."

Tramp and Lady were wandering down a path when suddenly they heard a shout. "Timber!"

They barely managed to scramble out of the way before a tree crashed onto the pavement. Tramp angrily poked his head up through the leaves.

"What hair-brained idiot—," he began to yell, but then stopped. A beaver was busy trimming the branches from the tree. Tramp had an idea. "Hey, there's the answer to our problem!" he told Lady.

Tramp walked up to the beaver, who was busily measuring the log with his tail.

"Pardon me, friend," said Tramp nonchalantly. "But I wonder if you'd do us a little favor."

"Too busy, sonny," the beaver said without looking up from his work. "Can't stop to gossip now."

"This'll take only a second," Tramp said.

The beaver shook his head. "Sorry, sonny, gotta haul this log down to the swamp." The beaver gave the log a shove, but it wouldn't budge. He pushed harder.

"Log hauling, huh?" Tramp mused aloud. He gave the beaver a friendly wink. "What you need is a log puller to help get the job done faster."

The beaver looked up, curious. "Did you say log puller?"

"Sure did," Tramp said in his smoothest salesman tone. "Here it is, modeled by the lovely lady. The New Improved Patented Handy-Dandy Never-Fail Little Giant Log Puller—the busy beaver's friend!"

The beaver stroked his chin and gave the contraption a considerable going-over.

"Can I try it on?" he asked at last.

"Help yourself," Tramp said agreeably. "All you have to do is place this strap between your teeth. . . ."

"Like this?" the beaver asked. Tramp smiled and nodded.

"And bite hard!"

The beaver did exactly as he was told.

"It's off!" Lady cried with relief. Tramp winked and motioned that it was time to get going.

"Wait a minute," the beaver said. Tramp froze. "I'll have to make certain it's satisfactory before we settle on a price."

"Ah, no, it's all yours, friend," Tramp said.

"Don't worry," Lady added. "It's a free sample."

"Free, huh?" said the beaver happily. "Well . . . thanks, thanks a lot."

The beaver resumed his log hauling, and Tramp breathed a sigh of relief. "Thanks, kid," he whispered to Lady. "That was quick thinking."

"I should be thanking you," Lady said. "I'd still be

wearing that muzzle if you hadn't thought of the Patented Handy-Dandy Never-Fail Little Giant Log Puller."

Tramp chuckled. "Just goes to show you. We may come from opposite sides of the tracks, but in some ways we have a lot in common."

CHAPTER SEVEN

IT WAS DARK by the time they got back to town. On the way Lady told Tramp the story of Aunt Sarah, the Siamese cats, and the muzzle.

"Say no more, I get the picture." Tramp nodded sympathetically. "That's what comes from tying yourself down to one family."

"Don't you have a family?" Lady asked as they strolled down the sidewalk under the glowing streetlamps.

"Sure, one for every day of the week," Tramp said. "The point is, none of them have me."

"I'm afraid I don't understand."

Tramp was about to explain when suddenly a wonderful aroma wafted toward them through the air. Tramp licked his lips. "Hey, something tells me it's suppertime. Come on, I'll show you what I mean."

He led Lady to a small clapboard house where a family was seated around the dining room table. "Now take the Schultzes here. Every Monday little Fritzie joins them for a great piece of Wiener schnitzel."

"Little Fritzie?" Lady asked.

"That's me," Tramp said with a wink. Next he led her to a wooden house a few doors down. "Now here at the O'Briens' is where little Mike has the world's best corned beef on Tuesdays."

"And you're little Mike?" Lady asked.

"You got it," said Tramp. "See, kid? When you're footloose and collar free, you take nothing but the best." He stopped and pricked up an ear. Lady could hear singing.

"Hey," Tramp said with obvious delight. "Tony's! The perfect place for a very special occasion. Come on."

Lady followed him to a brightly lit restaurant. The singing she heard was coming from inside. Lady started toward the front door.

"No, no," Tramp whispered. "This way. I have my own private entrance." He turned down an alley and around to the back of the restaurant. "Wait here," he said.

Lady watched from behind a wooden box as Tramp scratched at the back door of the restaurant.

"I'm coming," someone called from inside. A moment later a heavyset man wearing an apron appeared at the door. He looked around, then caught sight of Tramp.

"Hello, Butch!" he said. "Where you been, huh?" The man came out, and Tramp jumped up playfully and licked his face. The man laughed and turned back to the restaurant. "Hey, Joe," he said. "Bring some bones for Butch before he eats me up."

"Okay, Tony," Joe called from inside. "Some bones coming up."

Normally Tramp was quite happy with bones, but this being a special occasion, he was hoping for more elegant fare. He turned back to the box where Lady was waiting and barked loudly.

"What's this?" Tony asked curiously. When he saw Lady he smiled. "Hey, Joe, come have a look. Butch has a new girlfriend."

Joe came out, took a look at Lady, and grinned. "Well, son of a gun," he said. "Butch got himself a cocker spaniel."

Tony bent down and scratched Lady under the jaw. "And she's pretty sweet." He turned back to Tramp and spoke in a low voice. "You take my advice and settle down with this one, okay?"

Lady's ears perked up. She trotted over to Tramp. "*This* one?" she asked pointedly.

For Christmas, Darling receives a beautiful cocker spaniel puppy, which she names Lady.

Lady's proudest moment is when she gets her very own license.

Lady enjoys her comfortable life with Jim Dear and Darling.

Tramp revels in his carefree life as a footloose bachelor from the other side of the tracks.

Tramp tells Lady that when Jim Dear and Darling's new baby arrives it will mean nothing but trouble.

Lady is happy to welcome the new baby to her home.

When Aunt Sarah comes to baby-sit, she brings along her two cats, Si and Am.

Stop it! Lady barks when Si and Am attack the fish and the bird.

Aunt Sarah forces Lady to wear a muzzle.

It's up to Tramp to save Lady from a pack of snarling dogs!

Lady enjoys a romantic candlelit spaghetti dinner with Tramp.

Under the moonlight they make paw prints inside a giant heart.

Lady's dream night turns into a nightmare when she is picked up by the dogcatcher!

Lady angrily blames Tramp for all her troubles.

Trusty and Jock come to the rescue when Tramp is hauled away by the dogcatcher.

Tramp enjoys his first Christmas with Lady and his brand-new family.

Tramp blushed. "This one? Oh, uh . . . Tony doesn't mean anything by that. He's just joking."

Just then Tony returned with a small table and a red-and-white checkered tablecloth. "Now we fix you a table," he said, spreading it out. He put down bread-sticks and a candle.

Joe came out with a tray of bones. "Here are your bones, Tony."

Tony slapped the tray away. "Bones?" he shouted incredulously. "What's the matter with you?"

Joe shrugged.

"Tonight Butch gets the best in the house!" Joe muttered a hasty apology and scurried back into the kitchen. With exaggerated elegance Tony placed a menu on the table in front of Lady and Tramp. "Now tell me," Tony said. "What's your pleasure? À la carte? Or a full dinner?"

Taking his time, Tramp considered the menu carefully, then barked. Tony nodded crisply.

"Hey, Joe," he shouted. "Butch would like the spaghetti special, heavy on the meatballs."

Lady gazed admiringly at Tramp.

"Here you are," said Tony a few moments later. "The best spaghetti and meatballs in town."

Lady took a dainty bite. It was delicious! She was starting to feel glad that she'd met up with Tramp. Every moment with him was so exciting and new. Just when Lady thought the dinner couldn't be nicer, Tony and Joe strolled out playing an accordion and a mandolin. Tony sang a beautiful song about a beautiful night. "*This* beautiful night," Lady thought.

This is the night, it's a beautiful night
And we call it bella notte.
Look at the skies, they have stars in their eyes
On this lovely bella notte.
Side by side with your loved one, with your loved one
You'll find enchantment here.
The night will weave its magic spell when the one
    you love is near.
For this is the night, and the heavens are right
On this lovely bella notte.

Lady smiled. The stars, the music, the food, and Tramp, of course—it was all so wonderful. Lady was so enchanted she didn't notice they were eating the same strand of spaghetti until suddenly their noses touched! For an instant their eyes met. Lady pulled away shyly. Tramp nudged the last meatball to Lady's side of the plate. Lady gazed up into his eyes.

Later they strolled contentedly through the park and watched the moonlight sparkle on the lake. Tramp drew a heart in wet cement, and they each left a paw print inside the heart. Fireflies blinked here and there, and the stars twinkled in the sky. Lady stayed close to Tramp. Every time she looked into his eyes she felt her heart race. She had never felt this way before. Could it be love?

CHAPTER EIGHT

A ROOSTER CROWED, and Lady opened her eyes. It was morning, and she was lying beside Tramp on the top of a hill overlooking town. "Oh dear!" she gasped.

Tramp opened his eyes and yawned. "Something wrong?"

"I should have been home hours ago," Lady said primly.

"Aw, come on," said Tramp. "You still believe that faithful old dog routine? It's time you opened your eyes and saw what a dog's life can really be."

Lady gave him a confused look. Tramp stepped to the crest of the hill. "I'll show you what I mean." Lady walked up beside him. "Look down there and tell me what you see."

"I see nice homes with yards and fences," Lady said.

"Exactly," said Tramp. "Life inside fences. Life on a leash. Now look out there, past the town." Lady lifted her eyes and gazed out toward the horizon. "Look at the hills and mountains and that huge expanse of land. There's a great big hunk of world out there with no fence around it—a place where two dogs can find adventure and excitement. Who knows what wonderful experiences wait for us beyond those hills." He turned to Lady. "And it's all ours for the taking."

"It does sound wonderful," Lady admitted reluctantly. "But who'll watch the baby?"

Now it was Tramp's turn to look confused. He stared at her. The baby? From the look in her eyes Tramp knew there was nothing he could say that would change Lady's mind.

"Okay, come on," he said with a sigh. "I'll take you home."

As they walked back toward the world of leashes and fences, Tramp was disappointed that he hadn't been able to convince Lady to stay free with him. If only there was some way he could show her what a good time they'd have. They were passing a chicken coop when he got an idea.

"Hey," he said. "Ever chase chickens?"

"I should say not," answered Lady.

"Well," Tramp said, "then you haven't lived." He turned toward the chicken coop.

"But we shouldn't." Lady hesitated.

Tramp had a huge grin on his face. "I know." He started to dig under the fence around the coop. "That's what makes it fun. Come on, kid, it's time to start building some memories."

Lady hesitated again. "You're sure we won't hurt the chickens?"

"Naw," Tramp said. "I've done this plenty of times. We'll just stir 'em up a bit."

Lady stood outside and watched from a distance as Tramp quietly stepped into the henhouse. A moment later the air exploded with squawking chickens and flying feathers. Lady leapt out of the way as a whole flock of birds burst out of the henhouse, chased by Tramp.

"Some fun, huh, kid?" Tramp shouted gleefully.

Lady didn't see the fun in it at all. Suddenly she heard a loud blast. Tramp skidded to an abrupt stop. There was another blast. "What's going on in there?" came an angry voice.

"What was that?" Lady gasped.

"The signal to run!" Tramp yelled. "Come on!"

He dashed under the hole in the fence, and Lady followed. There was another shot. They ran down alleys and across yards. Lady was terrified. Tramp, however, was having the time of his life.

"Whee!" he cried as he leapt over a puddle. "This is living!"

Lady splashed through the puddle behind him and decided she honestly couldn't see what was so fun about being chased by an angry man with a gun. Tramp sprinted ahead, and Lady had a hard time keeping up. He turned a corner, and for a moment she lost sight of him. Then, from out of nowhere, a net came down tight around Lady's neck. Lady twisted and fought as best she could, but it was no use. She was trapped.

"So what have we here?" Lady looked up into the cruel face of the dogcatcher.

Meanwhile, Tramp had scooted around a billboard and stopped to catch his breath. "Now tell me that wasn't fun," he said. He looked around. He peered out from behind the billboard. "Hey, kid, where are you?" he called. No answer. He called again. Tramp backtracked all the way to the chicken coop, but there was no sign of Lady anywhere.

The dark green wagon pulled up in front of the pound. The dogcatcher came around to the back. "Come on," he said, reaching in to grab Lady. "It's time to get out."

Lady backed into a corner of the wagon. The

dogcatcher still managed to get hold of her and wrestled her out. The next thing Lady knew, she was being dragged down a dreary corridor lined with gloomy cages. Inside each cage, dogs stared out at Lady with sad, hopeless eyes. Lady felt terribly ashamed and very frightened.

The dogcatcher yanked open a door to one of the cages and pushed her inside. *Bang!* The door slammed shut behind her. Lady was so scared she trembled. Tears brimmed in her eyes. She felt so all alone.

"Hey, look, you guys," came a voice from the back of the cage. "Miss Park Avenue herself!"

Lady turned and found herself face-to-face with a motley-looking crew of canines. There were several mutts, a squat bulldog, a tall, gangly wolfhound, and a sleepy-eyed Chihuahua.

"A regular bloomin' debutante," said the bulldog with a laugh.

One of the mutts came up close to Lady and eyed her license. "Looks like the crown jewel you got there."

"What're ya in for, sweetheart?" the bulldog asked. "Puttin' fleas on the butler?"

They laughed scornfully. Lady began to back away. Just then a blue-eyed Pekingese pushed her way through the crowd.

"All right, you guys, lay off," she snapped.

"What's the matter, Peg?" the bulldog asked. "We was only havin' a bit of fun."

"Come on, Bull," Peg said. "Can't you see the poor kid's scared?"

"Pay no attention to them," the wolfhound told Lady.

"Boris is right," said Peg in a soothing voice. "They don't mean no real harm."

Lady was relieved. "But why were they picking on me?" she asked.

"It's your license," said Boris.

Lady was surprised. "What's wrong with it?"

"Nothing," Peg said. "It's your passport to freedom."

"Every dog in here would give his left hind leg for a license," said Boris.

"Without one," said a brown mutt, "it's just a matter of time until you take the long walk."

"What's that?" Lady asked.

The mutt jerked his muzzle toward the dogcatcher, who was leading a sickly-looking hound down the hall. "Through the one-way door," he said sadly.

Lady gasped. It wasn't fair, Lady thought. Just because they didn't have a license . . .

"Oh, well," Bull said with a sigh. "A short life, and a merry one. That's what Tramp always says."

Lady's ears perked up. Tramp? Did they know him, too?

Bull smiled and nodded at the thought. "Now there's a chap who'll never get caught," he said with real admiration and respect.

47

"You won't believe this, dearie," Peg told Lady, "but no matter how tight a jam he's in, that Tramp always finds a way out."

"Oh, I can believe that," Lady said, still angry that he had made her chase chickens.

"But even Tramp has his Achilles' heel," said Boris.

"Oh, yeah," said Bull. "The dames." He started to count on his paw. "Let's see now. There's been Lulu, and Trixie, and Fifi."

"And Rosita Chiquita," added the Chihuahua. "She's my sister."

Lady's eyes widened. There'd been so many!

"That Tramp," Peg said dreamily. "What a dog!"

"You tell 'em, Peg," Bull said.

"Yeah, that Tramp," said Toughy enviously. "He never takes the ladies seriously."

Well, Lady thought, *this* certainly is distressing news.

"But maybe someday he'll meet someone different," Boris said. "Some delicate, fragile creature whom he'll want to shelter and protect."

"Ya mean, like Miss Park Avenue?" Bull asked, nodding at Lady.

"Could be," Boris conceded. "But it's not all good news. You see, when he's under the spell of true love, he grows careless. And then the cossacks will finally pick him up."

"And it's curtains for Tramp," Toughy sighed.

48

The conversation was interrupted by the jiggle of a key in the cage lock. The dogcatcher stepped in. "All right, baby, they've come to take you home," he said, lifting Lady out. "You're too nice a girl to be in this place."

Thank goodness, Lady thought. She was saved. But she couldn't help feeling sorry for the others.

CHAPTER NINE

AUNT SARAH was not pleased. She gave Lady a harsh scolding and as punishment chained her to the dog-house outside. Lady was miserable.

Jock and Trusty couldn't help but notice how un-happy their friend was. Jock wished there was some-thing he could do for her. Then he had an idea. But it was going to take some coaxing to get Trusty to go along with his plan.

"Courage, courage," Jock whispered to Trusty as they walked up the path to Lady's doghouse.

"But I've never even considered matrimony," Trusty complained.

"Nor have I," said Jock. "But no matter which of us

she accepts, we'll always be the best of friends. And remember, not one word about her unfortunate experience. We don't want to hurt her feelings."

Lady was moping inside her doghouse when they arrived.

"Lassie?" Jock inquired softly.

"Please," Lady said forlornly. "I don't want to see anybody."

"But lassie," Jock said hopefully, "we've come with a proposition for helping you."

Lady looked up. "Helping me? How?"

Jock looked at Trusty and swallowed. "Well," he began nervously, "you see, lassie, neither of us is as young as we used to be."

"But we're still in the prime of life," added Trusty.

"And we've both got very comfortable homes," said Jock.

"Where we know you'll be welcome and appreciated," added Trusty.

Lady took a few steps out of her doghouse. She understood what they were trying to do, and it cheered her up despite everything that had happened. Lady knew she was lucky to have such good friends.

"So," Jock concluded, "if you could, uh, find it possible to, uh, to . . ."

"You're both very kind," she said, "and I do appreciate it, but—"

"Hey, kid!" came a familiar bark. Tramp squeezed

through a hole in the fence and trotted over with a big smile and a bone. "Hi, boys," he said to Jock and Trusty. "What's new at the kennel club?"

Jock, Trusty, and Lady turned their backs. The grin slid from Tramp's face. He laid the bone next to Lady. "Uh, a little something I picked up for you, kid."

Lady ignored him and walked as far away from him as the chain would allow.

"Looks like *I'm* the one who's in the doghouse," Tramp said woefully.

Trusty glared at him, then turned to Lady. "If this person is annoying you, Miss Lady—"

"We'll gladly throw the rascal out," Jock said.

"That won't be necessary, thank you," Lady replied.

"Very well, ma'am." Trusty and Jock decided it was time to go.

"You, you mongrel!" Jock snapped angrily at Tramp as he walked by. Tramp watched them walk away, then crawled over to Lady on his stomach.

"Aw, come on, kid," he said apologetically. "It wasn't my fault."

Lady was so angry all she could do was glower.

"I thought you were right behind me," Tramp explained. "Honest. And when I heard they'd taken you to the pound—"

Lady turned away. "Oh, don't even mention that horrible place! I was so embarrassed and frightened." Just the thought of it made her shiver.

"You shouldn't have been frightened," Tramp said. "Who could ever harm a cute little trick like you?"

Lady spun around. "Trick? That reminds me, who is Trixie?"

"Trixie?" Tramp repeated.

"And Lulu?" Lady asked angrily. "And Fifi? And Rosita Chiquita whatever her name is?"

"Oh, uh, yes, well, I can explain," Tramp stammered.

But Lady had no interest in his explanations. "I don't need you to shelter and protect me. As far as I'm concerned, you needn't worry about your heel."

"My heel?" Tramp asked, bewildered.

"And if you grow careless," Lady snapped, "don't blame me. I don't care if the cossacks do pick you up. Good-bye!" She kicked away the bone. "And you can take that with you!" With a huff she marched back into her doghouse.

Tramp could hear her crying inside the doghouse. He lowered his head sadly and walked away.

When Lady finally ran out of tears, she felt a little better. In fact, she wasn't even that angry at Tramp anymore. Maybe, she thought, she should forgive him. She stuck her head out of the doghouse, but the yard was empty. Tramp was gone.

53

CHAPTER TEN

IN THE DISTANCE Lady heard a clap of thunder, then the crackle of lightning. She sniffed the air. A storm was coming. Suddenly it began to rain.

In the woodpile, the rat stirred. Lady heard him scratching about, then saw him skulking along the edge of the garden, his hard little eyes glowing in the rain-spattered darkness. Lady growled and snarled. The rat skittered across the lawn and dashed for cover as Lady lunged. The chain snapped her back. The rat stopped to grin, then scampered up a vine-covered trellis toward the nursery.

Lady barked and howled.

A light went on in the upstairs window. The window slid open, and Aunt Sarah stuck her head out into the blowing wind and rain. "Stop that barking!" she yelled.

But the rat! Lady barked back. *It's in the nursery!*

"Stop that racket!" Aunt Sarah shouted again. "Hush! Hush!"

Lady yanked and pulled and tugged at her chain. She barked as loud as she could.

"Impossible dog!" Aunt Sarah slammed her window shut.

Lady was in a panic. The rat was in the nursery!

Just then Tramp trotted into the yard.

"I heard all the barking," he said. "What's wrong?"

"A rat!" Lady said. "Upstairs in the baby's room!"

"How do I get in?"

"There's a door on the back porch. Hurry!"

Tramp dashed onto the porch and through the doggy door. Inside, the house was as dark as coal. There was a crack and a sudden flash of lightning, and Tramp saw the stairs silhouetted in the light. He dashed up the steps and sniffed his way down the hall to the nursery. Tramp stopped. The door was ajar. He growled—he could smell the rat inside.

The rat was crouched at the foot of the crib. Tramp crept toward it and snarled. The rat turned and ran, and Tramp shot after it. They raced around and around the room. The rat bared its sharp teeth and flashed its razor-sharp claws. Tramp dodged and lunged. The rat sprang forward, ripping into Tramp's fur. Tramp lashed back. But the rat sank its claws tight into Tramp's fur, and Tramp howled.

Lady heard Tramp howl, and she jerked at the chain. It wouldn't budge. Lady strained against the chain as hard as she could. Suddenly it snapped loose. There was not a second to lose!

Lady raced up the stairway. There was a terrifying crash and a sudden burst of light, then an eerie silence. She stopped in the doorway. In the darkness she could hear breathing. Lightning crackled again, and Lady gasped as she saw the rat crawling along the banister of the baby's crib.

Nooooo! barked Lady.

Tramp leapt out from the darkness and caught the rat in his teeth and flung it across the room. The crib tipped and teetered and crashed to the floor. The baby! Lady thought. Tramp turned and dashed after the rat, which scampered under a dresser. Tramp dived at him and knocked a lamp to the floor. The rat dashed along the wall. Tramp pounced, snapping at the rat's tail and upending a table. Finally, the rat grew confused and entangled himself in the curtains. Now Tramp had him.

At the other end of the hall Aunt Sarah awoke with a start. She had heard a terrific crash and boom, but it wasn't thunder—it had come from the baby's room. "Good gracious!" she said, shooting straight up in her bed. The baby was crying! She hurried down the hall to the nursery and turned on the light.

"Merciful heavens!" Aunt Sarah shrieked. She rushed to the crib and scooped up the baby.

"Oh, you poor little darling," she said soothingly. "Now, now, thank goodness you're not hurt."

Aunt Sarah turned the crib right side up and settled the baby in it.

Lady and Tramp smiled at each other in relief.

Then Aunt Sarah turned to Tramp. "You vicious brute!" she snarled. She grabbed a broom and swung it. Tramp ducked and jumped backward. Aunt Sarah swung again and again. Before Tramp knew what had happened, he had backed himself into the closet. Aunt Sarah slammed the door shut. Tramp was locked in.

"The pound," Aunt Sarah decided. "That's it! I'll call the pound!"

No! Lady barked. *You don't understand! He saved the baby!*

Aunt Sarah grabbed the end of Lady's chain. "Come on!" she said. She pulled Lady down the stairs. "I'll call the pound this very minute. I couldn't sleep a wink with that brute in the house."

Lady tugged on the chain, but Aunt Sarah dragged her across the kitchen floor and forced her into the cellar. Lady scratched furiously at the locked door. She could hear Aunt Sarah on the telephone. "I don't care if you are alone there, young man," she said. "I insist you pick him up immediately!"

They'll take Tramp to the pound, Lady thought with a shiver of fright. And she remembered the wolfhound's words: *When Tramp is under the spell of true love, he grows careless. Then the cossacks will finally get him.*

No! she thought.

CHAPTER ELEVEN

JIM DEAR AND DARLING got off the streetcar at the corner. They'd had a delightful few days away, and now they were eager to get home to the baby. They walked down the rain-dampened sidewalk and noticed something odd. The dogcatcher's wagon was parked outside their house.

"What do you suppose?" Darling asked quizzically. She and Jim Dear quickened their pace. When they turned up the walk they met the dogcatcher, who was dragging a strange dog out of their house on a leash. Aunt Sarah stood on the porch with her hands on her hips.

"If you want my advice," she said, "you'll destroy that animal at once."

Jim Dear turned to the dogcatcher.

"Say, what's going on here?" he asked.

"Just picking up a stray," the dogcatcher said. "We've been after *this* one for months. Caught him attacking a baby."

"Good heavens!" Jim Dear gasped.

"My baby!" Darling cried. They rushed up the walk and into the house.

Jock and Trusty paused on the walk in front of the house.

"I was certain that dog was no good the first time I laid eyes on him," Jock told Trusty.

"Maybe," said Trusty, "but I never thought he'd do a thing like that."

Inside the house Aunt Sarah explained to Jim Dear and Darling, in grim detail, what she thought had happened. "Those dogs knocked over the crib. Thank goodness I got there in time to save the baby!"

"I'm sure there must be some mistake," Jim Dear said. "I know Lady would never do that."

In the cellar Lady heard his voice. *Thank goodness they've come home!* she barked. She scratched furiously at the cellar door until it opened.

"Lady, what are you doing in here?" Jim Dear said.

Lady raced excitedly around him, then sprinted up the stairs.

"Watch out!" Aunt Sarah cried. "That dog's loose! Keep her away from the baby!"

"Nonsense!" Jim Dear shouted, running up the stairs. "She's trying to tell us something."

Lady ran straight to the tangled curtain in the nursery and barked.

"What is it, old girl?" Jim Dear asked as he pulled back the curtains. "Darling! Aunt Sarah! Come here!"

Darling and Aunt Sarah rushed into the baby's room. Jim Dear showed Aunt Sarah what lay in the folds of the curtain. She shrieked and went pale as a ghost. "A rat!"

Waiting downstairs by the open front door, Trusty and Jock overheard what was said.

"We should've known," Trusty said regretfully.

"Aye," Jock said, looking down. "I misjudged him badly."

Trusty looked up. "We've got to stop that wagon!" he said with resolve.

"But we don't know which way they've gone," Jock said.

"We'll track 'em down," Trusty shouted. He bounded off the front porch and began sniffing.

Jock trotted after Trusty as they made their way down the muddy streets. They soon came to an intersection. Trusty stopped and sniffed in several directions.

"Now what?" Jock asked.

"The scent," Trusty mumbled as he sniffed. "Got to follow the scent."

Jock sighed and gave his old friend a sorrowful look. It was hopeless, he thought. "Let's face it," he said gently. "We both know you've lost your sense of smell."

Trusty raised his head in shock. He glowered at Jock. With renewed determination he resumed sniffing. Suddenly he howled loudly and tore off down the street. Jock had to scurry to keep up with him.

They came to a flooded intersection, and Jock felt his heart sink. Even a young bloodhound wouldn't be able to follow the scent through such deep water. It's no use! he thought again. Trusty splashed and sniffed, desperate to pick up the scent. Just when Jock was ready to give up, Trusty let out a great yowl. He'd found the scent! Well, well, Jock thought kindly. The old fella hasn't lost it, after all.

In the back of the dogcatcher's wagon Tramp heard the yowl and peered through the cage. "Well, doggone!" Tramp smiled appreciatively. But what could those two old codgers possibly do? he wondered.

Trusty decided to run ahead of the wagon and bring it to a stop. He barked furiously. The driver shouted and waved his arms. Trusty kept barking. The horse suddenly took fright and reared up. The wagon began to tip. CRASH! The wagon toppled over and came to a rest against a post.

A moment later a taxi carrying Jim Dear and Lady screeched to a stop. Jim Dear jumped out and explained to the dogcatcher how Tramp had saved the baby.

Frantic with worry, Lady ran to the back of the wagon to see if Tramp was all right. She found him and sighed.

"Hi, kid," he said with that same old carefree smile on his face. Lady had never been so happy to see another dog in her life. Just then she heard Jock whimper. Lady peered around the side of the wagon and saw Trusty lying beneath the broken wheel. Jock nudged his old friend, but Trusty didn't move. Lady's eyes filled with tears, and Jock howled mournfully into the night.

CHAPTER TWELVE

IT WAS CHRISTMAS AGAIN, exactly one year since Lady had first come to live with Jim Dear and Darling. Jim Dear was trying to get everyone to pose for a family portrait.

It wasn't easy. The family had grown considerably. There were Darling and the baby, who was crawling now. And there were Lady and Tramp—with four new pups of their own!

"All right, everybody," Jim Dear said from behind the camera. "Steady now. Hold it!" There was a great flash from the camera and a thick puff of smoke that sent Jim Dear rushing to open the window. As he did, he noticed two visitors coming up the icy front walk—

Jock in a new plaid sweater, and Trusty, limping gingerly on a broken leg.

Jim Dear held the door for them. "Merry Christmas, you two. Come in, come in. If you'll just step into the parlor, I'll see about refreshments." He turned to his wife. "Darling! Where'd you put the dog biscuits Aunt Sarah sent?"

"In the kitchen, Jim Dear," Darling replied.

While Jim Dear went to get the biscuits, Trusty and Jock joined Lady and Tramp.

"There's no doubt about it," Trusty said, studying the pups. "They've got their mother's eyes."

"But there's a little bit of their father in them, too," Jock said. He laughed as the pup who looked most like Tramp tugged playfully on his cardigan.

Tramp watched his family happily, his chest puffed out with pride. Jock was the first to notice that something new hung around his neck.

"Why, I see you finally acquired a collar," Jock said admiringly.

"Complete with a license," Tramp added.

"Caught the scent the moment I came into the house," said Trusty. He turned to the pups. "Of course, my sense of smell is very highly developed," he told them. "Runs in the family, you know."

Behind him, Jock sidled up to Lady and Tramp. "There'll be no living with him from now on," he whispered.

"As my grandpappy, Old Reliable, used to say . . ." Trusty paused. "Don't recollect if I've ever mentioned Old Reliable before."

"No, you haven't, Uncle Trusty," the pups chanted eagerly.

"I haven't?" Trusty was quite pleased. "Well, as Old Reliable used to say, uh, er, he'd say, uh, hummm . . ."

The four puppies wagged and thumped their tails excitedly.

"Well, he used to say," Trusty continued, "he used to say . . . uh, well . . ."

"What?" one of the pups asked impatiently.

Trusty frowned. "You know, I clean forgot what Old Reliable used to say."

Jock chuckled. Lady smiled and lay her head lovingly on Tramp's strong shoulder. It was going to be a wonderful Christmas. After all, they had a great deal to be merry about.